THE DAY THE
MOUNTAIN
BURST

by Louise Herman
illustrated by Giorgio Bacchin

Yes, I did survive that terrible event.

I'm an old man now and people still ask me about it. "Tell us, Marcus," they say. "Tell us about the lost city of Pompeii and the day the mountain burst." I have told the story many times, and believe me, it is fearsome enough to terrify children.

I do not usually put myself at the center of it, for I was certainly no hero. But the truth is that the eruption of Mount Vesuvius, which brought death to so many, brought something very different to me.

To explain the sort of boy I was, I must begin with my own beginning. I was born during the Great Earthquake, seventeen years before the disaster. The floor rolled and shook beneath my mother as she labored to give birth. When I gave a newborn's scream, my mother screamed too. But then she lay bloody and still. Tiles had dislodged and fallen from the ceiling to strike her dead.

My father hated me for it. I was cursed, he said, by Vulcan, the god of fire. Vulcan, who worked at his forge deep in the earth, had sent the earthquake and at the same time, had sent me to extinguish my mother's life. My father went away with the army and I never knew him.

My grandmother kept me. She also believed I killed my mother, but at least she fed and clothed me. When she died I was twelve, and her distant cousin Julius took me in. He was a smug, smiling, and prosperous man.

"You are lucky," he told me. "You have family to care for you even though you killed your mother."

Cousin Julius owned a large stable near the Nucerian Gate, where the rich men of Pompeii kept their horses or got horses for hire. He put me to work as a messenger. From dawn to dusk, I ran all over the city, led horses to their owners, and brought them back.

Cousin Julius had slaves to brush and feed the horses, but he worked me harder than any of them, all the time reminding me how lucky I was. "Even though you were cursed, you're still family," he pointed out again and again.

I was family, but I saw little of Julius's wife and children. His wife spent all day gossiping with friends. The children teased me at first, then lost interest as we all grew older. They had their lessons; the boys idled at baths and taverns; and the girls shopped and dressed and arranged their hair.

The youngest daughter, Livia, was lively and dainty and not as spoiled as the others. I loved her from the day I first saw her, but it was clear Julius would never let me try to win her.

I was family, but there were no lessons for me, no music or poetry or philosophy. Cousin Julius taught me to write and calculate just enough to help with the accounts.

I was family, so he did not make me eat with the slaves, but I rarely had leisure to eat with the family. I got the remains of their dinner from the old Greek kitchen slave.

So, at the time of the disaster I was a skinny youth with a mean face and a bitter heart. I hated Cousin Julius. I obeyed him and never stole from him, but only because I didn't want to give him the satisfaction of beating me. I detested his self-satisfied smile.

I disliked his wife and sons, too, for their easy days. I had contempt for the rich men whose horses I led around. I hated what my father called my curse. My life tasted like a hard, bitter olive. I had no friends, not unless you counted Despina, the old Greek cook. But she was losing her memory, and half the time she made no sense.

Was there any living thing I loved? Yes, I loved the beautiful, muscular horses that cared nothing for curses. And I loved Livia, but hopelessly.

I had been out early, that day the mountain burst, and came into Despina's kitchen for a break from the hot summer sun and maybe a bite to eat. "The stove is smoking," she said as she brought me bread and soup.

"The stove?" I said. "But it's not lit, Despina. Not in this heat."

She only said again, "Smoking."

When I returned to the stable I found the slaves in the yard gazing up at the peak of the mountain, where a narrow column of smoke could be seen rising into the sky. They had felt tremors; they had heard a thunderclap. If Vulcan was active at his forge under the mountain, we could have another earthquake.

The slaves looked uneasily at me, no doubt thinking of my curse. I ignored them and went on with my work. The column of smoke got thicker and plumed at the top. The sky slowly darkened, and gray ash began to fall. Folks were afraid, and soon families with bundles began to leave the city by our gate.

Some men sent for their horses, but most of our neighbors waited and watched. The mountain has smoked before, they said. It won't last, it will come to nothing. The ash is light.

Light it was, but it continued to fall. When an inch or two had accumulated, Cousin Julius decided to remove his wife and children to their country house near Nuceria.

Naturally Cousin Julius did not admit he was afraid. The ash meant nothing, he insisted. It was merely unpleasant. They would leave until it ceased and the slaves could sweep it away.

"You stay here, Marcus," he said. "Take care of the horses. If there is civic disorder, keep looters out of the house."

He prepared two carts. Though he scoffed at the danger, I noticed he packed bags of coins, his wife's jewelry, and all their other gold and silver possessions. While his sons harnessed horses to the carts, his wife and older daughters came outside through the ash on tiptoe, with capes over their heads.

Where was Livia? She had gone that morning to see her friend Flavia. Julius dispatched a slave to fetch her, but the slave did not return, and Julius finally said, "We'll stop for her on the way."

He took the remaining slaves, except for old Despina. "She's not worth the trouble," I heard him tell his wife. "We'll hire a cook in Nuceria."

The carts rolled away, leaving deep lines in the ash.

I stepped into the kitchen. Despina said, "Where are they?"

"They've gone to the country house in Nuceria."

"But they should have told me. I cooked."

"They did tell you, Despina. You forgot."

I heard a shout and returned to the stable, where a man had come for his horse. Another family escaping the city. I relocked the stable and returned to the kitchen.

"Where are they?" Despina asked.

"Gone to the country house, Despina, I told you."

But again I was summoned to the stable, and when I returned to the kitchen I noticed tiny pebbles falling with the ash, like dirty foam made of rock, scarcely heavier than bits of dry bread. Things were getting worse. Should I take the horses and follow Julius?

Despina asked, "Where are they?"

"The country house, Despina," I said, exasperated.

"Her too? The mistress?"

"Her too."

"Is she your mother?"

"No, she is certainly not my mother."

"Am I your mother?"

"No, Despina. My mother died when I was born. You know that."

Despina narrowed her eyes. "We must find our mothers where we can."

I shook my head. Poor old fool. I opened the door to return to the stable.

"Some of my people," Despina went on, "believe the Earth is our mother."

"Well, Despina, my people believe in the god Vulcan, and right now I'm worried about what Vulcan is doing in his forge, down inside your Mother Earth."

"Vulcan. The god who blessed you."

"Cursed me, you mean."

She shrugged. "It seems a blessing to me. You have never had a happy day in your life, yet he has made you as strong as iron."

I could not think what to say, so I walked out and left her.

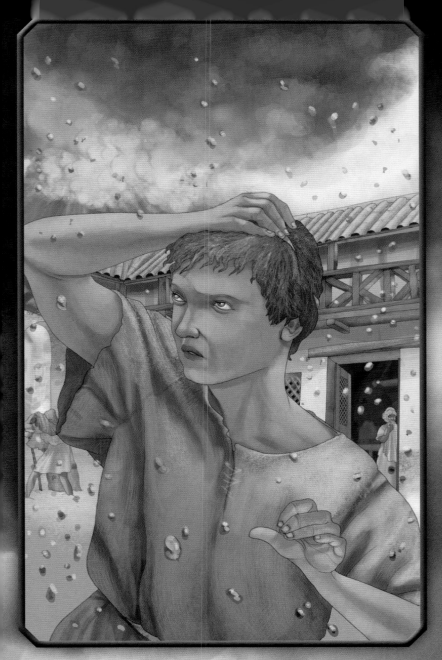

The light, falling bits of rock were larger now, the size of coins. They stung my face. The ash was over my ankles. A slave came for his master's horses, coughing and shaking with fear. He had seen a dead man in the street. An old man, choked by the ash. I hurried back to the kitchen.

Despina began, "Where are—" but I interrupted. "The ash is falling harder. It's choking people. We should go."

She was confused and frightened. "You go. I must cook."

Just then I heard a sharp cry: "Marcus! Marcus! Are you here?" It was a girl's voice. A familiar voice. A voice I loved.

"Livia!" I ran out to the road. She was in a loaded cart with her friend Flavia and Flavia's brother. "Your father left an hour ago," I said. "Did he not come for you?"

"He thought we had gone on ahead. We'll catch up with them. But I hoped you were still here. How many horses are left?"

"Only three."

"Bring them."

I hesitated. "You mean...?"

"Yes, yes, we have room. Hurry, get the horses."

I unlocked the stable door with fumbling hands and went inside. She had come for me! I couldn't believe it. The mountain was raining ash, and she had come for me especially.

I hurried to put bridles on two of the horses and led them outside, where they stumbled in the stone-filled ash. I tethered them to her cart.

"Now the other," she said. "Quick."

"I'll call Despina. She's in the kitchen."

But Livia said. "Oh, forget her. She's too old to make this trip. Just get the other horse."

I ran for the last horse, a gentle old mare. Her eyes rolled with fear at the falling stones.

"Hurry!" called Livia again. Her friend's brother commanded his horses and the cart began to roll. I followed it to the gate, murmuring to the mare to calm her.

But as we went through, I felt my steps slow.

I could not leave that poor old woman behind. I stopped.

"Come on, Marcus!" cried Livia. "What's wrong with you?"

Livia looked at the old mare. Then, without a word, she turned away. The cart rolled on.

I understood. She had come for the horses. She wanted me only to unlock the stable. The old mare was like Despina, not worth the trouble. And neither, in the end, was I.

Despina had come out into the yard, and stood watching with her palms turned up as the little stones struck her. The ash made her cough and gasp for breath. "Go," she said.

But I pulled her into the kitchen. I found cloths and folded them and tied them on her head and my own. I gave her a cloth to hold over her nose. I had no appetite for food or drink, but I tied up what I could find in a bundle.

Somehow I hoisted Despina's old body up onto the mare, and she clung to the creature's mane, though she could not speak for choking. I led the horse out through the gate. It was dark as dusk, though sunset was hours away. The ash on the ground was deeper than my knees, and some falling rocks were nearly the size of my fist.

I can hardly describe the misery of the next few hours and the horrors we saw. Hundreds were fleeing the city, in carts or on foot, with torches and clumsy head coverings, ghostly and covered with ash. We saw dozens of dead, abandoned where they lay. They had choked in the ashy air, or their hearts had failed, or they were crushed under cart wheels.

Our horse struggled, and I wore myself out kicking away the ash in front of her. On we plodded, step after step, for an eternity.

By sunset we were far enough from the mountain that the ash was less thick and we no longer felt the stones strike us. We paused at a fork in the road. I helped Despina down from the horse to stretch herself.

"Where are they?" she said.

Wearily I said, "At the country house in Nuceria."

"Which way is it?"

I pointed. "This way, to the south."

She looked me in the eye, and then she turned her back on the way I had pointed out. "We must go this way, then." Deliberately and determinedly she began to march along the opposite road, to the northeast.

Thus, in her simple way, she gave us our freedom.

I wish I could say the worst was over then, but it was not so. The old mare went first. Her legs gave out under her; she crumpled to the ground and died. There was a little grove nearby where people had made a fire. Despina and I staggered there and collapsed into exhausted sleep.

I woke at first light to find Despina dead beside me. Having no means to bury her, I wrapped her in the cloths from our head coverings, and left her where she lay.

My new road led along a ridge, from which I saw Vesuvius lost in a deep black cloud. A vast torrent of boiling ash and rock had burst from the top and poured down over Pompeii, burying the city and all living things that remained there.

Much later I learned that Julius had survived the journey to Nuceria, but Livia was never heard from again. As for myself, I eventually arrived in Rome and found work at a forge. In time I became a master metal worker, a true son of Vulcan. I married well and fathered six fine children.

Every year I visit that dusty fork in the road near Nuceria, which I honor as the gravesite of my mother.

Of course I do not like to say this to people, but the truth is that since the eruption of Vesuvius, I have been a happy man.